Caroline jumped out of bed. She joined her brothers at the window. Mother was holding a torch and checking to see if the vegetables were freezing. Caroline knew that if vegetables froze before they were picked, they would rot.

"I'm going to help, too!" Caroline said, her teeth chattering.

"Get back to bed before you catch cold, Caroline," Joseph said sternly. "Henry and I will help Mother. I don't want you going out. You're too little."

Caroline knew that Joseph would not change his mind. He and Henry would help Mother, and she knew she was too little to be of use in the garden at night. Still, it was maddening to be too young all the time. Why couldn't she be the oldest for a change?

BE SURE TO READ OTHER BOOKS IN

THE LITTLE HOUSE FAMILY

THE MARTHA YEARS

Laura's great-grandmother, born 1782

LITTLE HOUSE IN THE HIGHLANDS

THE CHARLOTTE YEARS

Laura's grandmother, born 1809

LITTLE HOUSE BY BOSTON BAY

THE LAURA YEARS

America's Original Pioneer Girl, born 1867

LITTLE HOUSE IN THE BIG WOODS

FARMER BOY

LITTLE HOUSE ON THE PRAIRIE

ON THE BANKS OF PLUM CREEK

BY THE SHORES OF SILVER LAKE

THE LONG WINTER

LITTLE TOWN ON THE PRAIRIE

THESE HAPPY GOLDEN YEARS

THE FIRST FOUR YEARS

By Cynthia Rylant:

OLD TOWN IN THE GREEN GROVES
Laura Ingalls Wilder's Lost
Little House Years

The Rose Years
Laura's daughter, born 1886
LITTLE HOUSE ON ROCKY RIDGE

LITTLE HOUSE IN BROOKFIELD

by MARIA D. WILKES

HarperTrophy®
An Imprint of HarperCollins*Publishers*

HarperCollins®, ®, Little House®, and The Caroline Years™ are trademarks of HarperCollins Publishers.

 For information address HarperCollins Children's Books, a division of HarperCollins Publishers, 1350 Avenue of the Americas, New York, NY 10019.
www.littlehousebooks.com

Library of Congress Cataloging-in-Publication Data
Wilkes, Maria D.
Little house in Brookfield / Maria D. Wilkes. — 1st abridged ed.
p. cm.
Summary: An abridged version of the story of young Caroline Quiner, who would grow up to become Laura Ingalls Wilder's mother, and her family surviving their first year without Father in the frontier town of Brookfield, Wisconsin.
ISBN-10: 0-06-114821-0 (pbk.)
ISBN-13: 978-0-06-114821-7 (pbk.)
1. Ingalls, Caroline Lake Quiner—Juvenile fiction. [1. Ingalls, Caroline Lake Quiner—Fiction. 2. Wilder, Laura Ingalls, 1867–1957—Family—Fiction. 3. Frontier and pioneer life—Wisconsin—Fiction. 4. Wisconsin—Fiction. 5. Family life—Wisconsin—Fiction.] I. Title.
PZ7.W648389Li 2007 2006103556
[Fic]—dc22 CIP
AC

Typography by Christopher Stengel

❖

First Harper Trophy Edition, 1996
Abridged Harper Trophy Edition, 2007

To Peter,
Who makes the thoughts clearer,
the words truer,
the moments richer.

LITTLE HOUSE IN BROOKFIELD

Inside

Caroline woke up. Pointing her toes under the sheet, she stretched her arms above her head as high as she could.

"Caroline!" Four-year-old Eliza tugged on Caroline's nightdress.

Caroline put her finger to her lips. "Hush!" she whispered. "You'll wake Martha!"

Martha, asleep on the other side of Eliza, had the sheet pulled right up to her chin. Martha was the oldest of the three Quiner girls, at nine.

Hazy shafts of light were spilling through

the window. Caroline sat up and inched her way to the foot of the bed. She looked around the curtain that cut the room in two. Her brothers, Joseph and Henry, were not yet awake.

But Mother was. Her footsteps sounded back and forth across the wooden floor in the kitchen below. Fat pork was sizzling in the frying pan, and the sweet smell of hotcakes filled the house.

Mother's footsteps became louder and louder. She was climbing the stairs. Her face rose through the opening in the attic floor. "Good morning, girls," Mother said.

Every morning, Mother looked at the girls' bed first, knowing Caroline would be awake and ready to waken the others. Caroline loved helping Mother and making her smile. Especially now, when Mother didn't smile nearly as much as she used to.

"Good morning, Mother," Caroline said.

"Time to wake everyone, Caroline. The sun's already rising, and the morning's wasting." Mother disappeared down the stairs.

Caroline reached over Eliza and shook Martha's arm. "Mother says to wake up, Martha."

Martha pulled the sheet over her head and grumbled, "Hush, Caroline. It's time to sleep." This is what Martha said every morning. She did not like waking up.

Caroline climbed out of bed. The wooden boards were cool under her bare feet. She pushed the curtain aside and tiptoed over to the boys' bed. Gently she shook Henry.

Henry sat up, startled. Then he saw Caroline. "Morning already, little Brownbraid?" he yawned.

Ever since she was three years old, Caroline had been called "little Brownbraid." One morning Mother had twisted Caroline's thick, soft hair into a long brown braid. Father noticed it at breakfast and said, "How pretty you are, little Brownbraid!" and that became his special name for her.

Caroline missed Father. He had been gone for almost a whole year. He had sailed away on a big boat called a schooner, and he had never come back. Mother said Father was in heaven. Caroline knew heaven was wonderful, but she still wished Father was at home.

Henry shoved Joseph as Caroline pulled the curtain behind her. In a few minutes, the floorboards creaked and shook as the boys thundered down the stairs.

Caroline shook Martha's arm again. "Wake up!"

Martha threw the quilt back. "All right, all right," she said. "I'm awake."

Reaching up to the wooden pegs that were spaced out along the wall, Caroline took down dresses for her and Eliza. Eliza squirmed out of her nightgown, and Caroline buttoned her into her clothes. After dressing herself, Caroline turned her back to Martha and waited impatiently as Martha sleepily fastened the long row of buttons.

"Hurry, Martha," Caroline said.

"It's too early to hurry."

Caroline didn't think it was too early. She

wanted to eat the hotcakes.

Hotcakes were her very favorite. She loved to drop a pat of butter on the steaming cakes and watch it melt and slide from the top round cake right down to the bottom. Then she'd pour sugar syrup over the top of the stack and eat them before the syrup ever had a chance to drizzle off the hotcakes onto her plate. Her stomach rumbled just imagining it.

As soon as Martha had finished, Caroline buttoned up Martha's dress. Then they braided each other's hair. Finally they could go downstairs.

"I hope Henry hasn't eaten all the hotcakes," said Caroline.

The fire in the hearth hissed and popped, and the kitchen glowed with early-morning sunshine that poured in through the windowpanes. Grandma rocked slowly in front of the fire, singing softly to baby Thomas and bouncing him on her knees.

"Good morning, Grandma," Caroline and Martha sang out.

"Good morning, dears." Grandma smiled. The rocking chair groaned and continued rocking as she stood up. Pulling a hairbrush from her apron pocket, she beckoned to the girls. "Come. Let's braid your hair so you'll be all ready for breakfast."

One by one, Caroline, Eliza, and Martha sat on Grandma's lap as she brushed and braided their hair. Martha and Eliza had two braids each. Only Caroline had one long braid.

Joseph was bending over the hearth. He lifted the kettle of water from the fire and walked toward the washstand. Carefully, he tipped the kettle over the washbasin. Caroline was always afraid that the kettle would drop and its steaming water would splash all over the floor. It was so heavy! Once, when the kettle was empty and cold and sitting on the floor far away from the fire, Joseph had allowed Caroline to try and lift it. No matter how hard she had pulled, the kettle wouldn't budge.

Joseph finished filling the washbasin. Caroline dipped her hand into the soft soap and washed her face and hands with the hot water. She had just finished cleaning Eliza's face when the kitchen door flew open. Henry burst into the room, carrying a load of cordwood that almost reached his eyes.

"I'm hungry!" Henry shouted as he dropped the logs in front of the wood box.

"We have a lot more wood to fetch before we eat, Henry," Joseph said. He was two years older than Henry and always told him what to do.

"It can wait until after breakfast," Mother decided. "Wash up, boys."

Caroline now helped Martha set the table. Martha handed the tin plates and cups to Caroline, who placed them around the table in front of each chair. Baby Thomas was too little to sit at the table. He would stay in the settle, where he could see everyone and stay out of harm's way.

Mother carried the platter of hotcakes and crisp fat pork slices from the stove to the table. Grandma filled each cup with milk. Martha set a big bowl of applesauce and a crock of butter in the center of the table. Caroline waited impatiently, trying hard not to look at the tall, steaming stack of hotcakes.

The very last thing Mother put on the table was the sugar syrup. Now they all sat down. Each head bowed as Mother prayed. "For this meal we are thankful, Lord. Amen."

Hotcakes and applesauce, butter and sugar syrup were passed from hand to waiting hand. Caroline put a pat of sweet butter on her hotcakes and then poured sugar syrup on top. She waited until the butter had melted over the sides of the hotcakes and when she could not wait any more, she ate.

"Henry, give some of that to Eliza," Mother warned as Henry dropped a large dollop of sweet butter on his hotcakes. Caroline looked at Henry's plate and hoped that she wouldn't have to share any of her butter with Eliza. It was too delicious. Grudgingly, Henry spread a tiny pat of his butter on Eliza's hotcake and observed, "I didn't take nearly as much as Father used to, Mother."

Mother's eyes were suddenly sad as she

looked across the table at Henry. "I certainly hope that you don't *ever* eat as much butter as your father did, Henry," she replied. "Why, we'd never be able to keep any fresh butter in the house!"

"Mother, please tell the story about the day Grandma caught Father eating her biscuits!" Martha pleaded.

"I think you should ask Grandma to tell you that story, Martha," Mother answered. "After all, she was there when it happened."

"Oh yes, please, Grandma, tell us!" Caroline begged.

"Are you certain, Charlotte?" Grandma asked.

"Of course."

Grandma began speaking in her soft voice, and Caroline stopped eating so she could pay proper attention. Stories about Father were the only thing she liked better than hotcakes.

"When your father was a boy, not much bigger than you, why, he loved hot biscuits more than anything. Whenever I'd bake fresh biscuits, I'd set them out on the table to cool.

At suppertime, we'd pass the biscuits around, and even though I knew I had baked a dozen, there were always only eleven biscuits in the basket. And when we'd pass the fresh butter, a good chunk was always missing from the beautiful butter print I had worked so hard to make! Every time I baked, both biscuits and butter were missing. And no one ever knew where they had gone.

"One day, I decided to catch the biscuit thief. I stood behind the door in the kitchen and watched as your father crawled across the floor in his knickers. He went right under the table, reached up, and felt around for the basket of biscuits. When he found it, he grabbed a biscuit. Then he reached up for the butter, broke a piece off, rubbed the butter on the biscuit, and popped it in his mouth."

"What did you do, Grandma?" Martha asked, her fork in midair.

"I marched right over to the table and stood in front of him. You can be sure that he crawled out from under the table right quick. I said, 'Young Henry, why have you been taking these biscuits?' "

"What did Father say?" Caroline asked eagerly.

"He said, 'I can't eat the butter all by itself, Mama, can I?' "

Henry laughed out loud. "Did he get in trouble, Grandma?"

"Well, young Henry," Grandma said, "he didn't eat any biscuits or butter for a whole month."

"A whole month?" Henry asked. Grandma nodded. Without another word, Henry spread some more of his butter on Eliza's hotcakes.

"Thank you, Henry," Mother said.

"A whole month without any butter!" Caroline thought, amazed.

Breakfast ended soon after Grandmother Quiner's story, as there were chores to do. Mother pulled a chair next to Thomas and sat down to sew. Joseph and Henry went to gather more wood for the fire. Martha washed the dishes. Caroline was only six years old, and too little to wash the dishes, but she could dry them.

Next was their bedroom. "I wish *I* could bring in wood instead of make beds," Martha said as she and Caroline climbed the stairs. Caroline was glad that she didn't have to bring in wood. Joseph and Henry always had bits of wood in their clothes. Caroline didn't like her dress to get all dirty.

Caroline evened out the bumps in the mattress where pockets of straw had bunched up during the night. Once the mattress was flat again, she smoothed the sheet over it. Martha flung their quilt up in the air and let it float back down onto the bed. Caroline and Martha shook the pillows until they were fluffy again and set them neatly at the head of the bed.

Then, while Martha straightened the boys' side, Caroline swept the floor with the tall broom from the kitchen.

"Done!" Martha said as she shook out the last pillow. "I'm all finished, and I can't wait to get outside!"

Caroline was also eager to go. The chickens

were waiting to be fed. "I'm finished, too," she said. With one last look around, she followed Martha downstairs, set the broom back in its corner, and ran out the door.

Outside

The sun was beginning its climb to the top of a cloudless blue sky as Caroline followed Martha into the yard to do their outside chores. The morning chorus of robins' songs that greeted them was interrupted by the loud splitting of logs.

Martha went off to the barn, and Caroline ran past the woodpile, where Henry and Joseph were busy chopping wood. They raised their axes high above their heads and brought them crashing down. *CRACK*! went the logs.

Caroline slowed down as she reached the

garden that covered half of their acre of la
Rows of corn towered in front of her, thei
green leaves flopping like rabbits' ears. Lifting the bottom of her dress, Caroline stepped over the stick fence that surrounded the garden. It had taken days for her and Martha to find more of the sticks that Father and Joseph had used to build that fence. They needed to make it strong to keep the wild animals out.

Pushing her way through the corn, Caroline searched until she found a thick ear. She pulled back its husk, just far enough to look at the first few kernels of corn.

"How's it look, little Brownbraid?"

Caroline turned. Henry's face peered at her between the tall stalks.

Every morning before she fed the chickens, Caroline checked a few pieces of the late-summer ears to see if they were ripe, and every morning Henry waited at the end of a row to find out if the corn was ready, because he just couldn't wait to eat it. Caroline couldn't wait for the kernels to be plump and yellow, either. Corn was her favorite vegetable, and they

for dinner or supper since they and eaten their first crop three

too small," Caroline called out smoothing the husk back over the ear. e by the end of the week!" Henry said hopefully. His head disappeared, and the stalks he had been holding snapped back together.

Leaving the tall cornstalks, Caroline walked through the rest of the garden. There were potatoes, onions, turnips, carrots, and sweet potatoes. Each bushy plant was hiding a vegetable that grew under the ground. Father once told her that these vegetables didn't grow in the sunshine, but Caroline couldn't imagine how you could grow if you were buried in dirt.

Caroline climbed back over the stick fence and headed for the barn. The yard was covered with thick clusters of tall grass and wildflowers. The petals of the cowslips bent backward, their yellow tips pointing straight to the sky. Bunches of tiny white flowers hid the snakeroot that hugged the ground.

The barn stood behind the frame house,

past the woodpile and the garden. Until Caroline was three years old, the barn had been a log cabin. The whole family had lived there—everyone except for baby Thomas, who hadn't yet been born. When Caroline was four years old, Father and some neighbors built a frame house close to the road. The Quiners left the little log cabin and moved into the frame house, and the log cabin became the barn. Even though tools and grain and hay were stored there now, Caroline still felt like the barn was her home.

Sunlight rushed into the center room as she pulled the barn door open. She took a deep breath and filled her lungs with the sweet smell of the fresh hay that was in the loft above her head. When the barn had been their log cabin, she had slept in the loft. Now it held only straw.

Caroline went to the back of the barn, where Mother had once cooked their meals. Some baskets and two large buckets were stored there, and Caroline picked up one of each and headed to the grain bin that was set against one wall. Joseph and Henry kept the big wooden bin filled with grain for the animals. The lid was very heavy in order to keep the mice from getting in and eating all the feed. Caroline could not lift the lid last year when Father was alive. She wished Father knew she was now big enough to lift it all by herself.

Caroline began filling the bucket with grain. After she filled half of the bucket, she pulled the lid of the feed bin away from the wall and stepped back as it fell into place with a thud. A puff of grain dust rose in the air. Picking up the bucket of grain and her empty basket, Caroline headed back into the sunshine and around the corner to the henhouse.

A wooden peg on the door kept the henhouse safe from foxes and wild dogs. Caroline twisted the peg and the door dropped to the ground, making a slope for the hens. "Morning, hens!" she called.

Scooping a handful of grain from the bucket, she scattered it in front of the henhouse. The hens poked their brown- and gold-feathered heads out of their house and immediately began squawking at Caroline. They hopped and fluttered down the door-slope and onto the ground. They waddled and clucked, their red crowns bobbing up and down as they picked at the kernels of grain and scratched in the dirt for bugs and seeds.

While the chickens were eating, Caroline looked in the henhouse at the slatted nesting boxes that sat on the shelf. She reached inside and ran her fingers through the straw in each box. The straw scratched and tickled her fingers as she searched for eggs. One, two, three. Four. Five! Five eggs!

Caroline tugged some tall grass from the ground and made a small green nest in the empty basket. Carefully she took each egg out of its nesting box and cushioned it in the soft grass. Caroline smiled proudly and hurried back toward the house, holding her nest of eggs tightly. Five whole eggs! Mother would be so pleased.

General Store

Summer eased into fall, and Caroline began to spend the chilly afternoons sitting at the sewing table and practicing her stitches with Grandma. She knew five different stitches already: cross-stitch, slip stitch, backstitch, running stitch, and the one she liked best, daisy stitch. She was quick and neat when she pulled the needle through the rough cloth. She almost never pricked her fingers—not like Martha, whose sampler was dotted with blood.

Caroline had sewed *A, B, C,* and *D* each

in a different stitch. She was now partway through *E*.

"Caroline, it's time to go now," said Mother. This afternoon Mother, Henry, and Caroline were going to town. Caroline liked sewing but she liked going to town even more.

Grandma looked up from her needlepoint. "You're leaving for town now, Charlotte?" she asked.

"Yes, Mother Quiner," Mother answered. She picked up an empty jug and basket lying next to the dish dresser and set them on a chair beside the sewing table. "I've called Martha in to help with Eliza and Thomas."

Folding the cloth in half with the stitched letters on the inside, Caroline handed it to Grandma with her needle and thread. "Thank you, Grandma," she said, and ran up to her room to get her white bonnet from the chest.

Caroline hadn't been to town since the springtime. Even though it was only two miles from the Quiners' house, Mother visited town far less often than Father used to. "Too crowded!" Mother would say whenever she returned from a trip to town. But Father had always loved the hustle and bustle, and he had often taken Caroline along with him.

"This town's grown up the same as you, Caroline," he'd tell her as they arrived at the crossroads of the two main roads in Brookfield. Shaking his head, Father would marvel at the cluster of houses and shops. "The day you were born, there weren't but a hundred folks or so in this part of Wisconsin," he'd say. "There's ten times that now. Just look at it! A regular little town!" Caroline would then feel Father's gentle tug on her braid. "With any luck, you won't grow up quite so fast, my little Brownbraid."

Caroline tied her bonnet strings tightly beneath her chin, kissed Grandma on the cheek, and followed Mother out the door.

Though the sunshine was warm, there was a crisp autumn breeze that chilled her cheeks. Caroline was glad that she was wearing her blue wool dress with long sleeves.

Henry emerged from the back of the house, carrying a heavy burlap sack. Caroline knew it was filled with ashes from their fireplace. Mother would trade the ashes for food and supplies, and the grocer would have the ashes made into soap that he would sell to other customers.

The three of them walked down the dirt road, past several frame houses. Like the Quiners, many of their neighbors had built new houses close to the road and now used their old log cabins as barns and stables.

Dry leaves danced all along the road. Caroline heard them crunching beneath her feet and remembered how much Father had loved walking on the autumn leaves and listening to them crackle. The last time the leaves had dropped, Father had left on his voyage. Caroline struggled to keep tears from slipping down her cheeks and tried to think about how exciting it was to be heading to town.

"Johnny O'Leary, move that log away now!" A loud, angry voice made Caroline jump and forget her sadness at once. They had just arrived at the crossroads of town, and everything was screaming and jumping and hurrying all around them. A large group of men, busy building a new structure on one corner, half listened as a burly man with a stubbly beard barked orders at them. Some of the men were chopping and splitting wood; others were hauling stone. The noise was deafening, and Caroline clapped her hands over her ears. Never before had the town seemed so loud and busy. Caroline moved closer to Mother and hurried along behind her, her shoes now kicking up dust instead of crunching leaves.

"Goodness glory!" Mother raised her voice so she could be heard above the chopping axes and crashing stones. "Another tavern! What we need in this town is another schoolhouse!"

Mother started across the busy street, but then stopped so suddenly that Caroline almost crashed into her. A thunderous roar shook the street.

"Stay where you are, children," Mother said.

"What is it?" Caroline asked, struggling to see around Mother.

"It's the stagecoach!" Henry shouted.

The dust from the road swirled up in thick,

choking gray clouds. Six huge horses snorted and strained as they pulled the coach past the Quiners. Caroline stared up in wonder.

"Who-o-o-o-a! Who-o-o-o-a!"

Caroline jumped, and all at once the team of horses stopped.

The stagecoach now stood directly in front of her. She had seen stagecoaches on her trips to town before, but she had never been so close to one. The front wheel was as tall as she was, and the back wheel was even taller. Thick leather straps were slung over the axles, and between the wheels, the coach hung, looking like a huge, brown wooden box. Its flat top was loaded with people and luggage. A black-bearded man was seated on top of the coach, right in front. Two other men sat with him, one on either side.

"Stop! Brookfield!" the black-bearded man called out. He was the driver. It was his voice that had shouted at the horses to "Whoa."

The driver jumped from the top of the coach. He opened the coach door right in front of Caroline, and she stood on her tiptoes to peek inside. Benches at the front and back were packed tight with passengers. More passengers sat on a third bench in the middle of the coach.

The passengers began pouring out. Men in suit coats and wide-brimmed hats jumped out into the street first. Some turned back to help the women in their long dresses step down from the coach.

"Baggage!" the driver bellowed. He climbed to the top of the stagecoach and began handing down the bags to the waiting passengers.

One short woman wearing a long black coat and a fancy black hat chattered loudly to her companion as they waited for their bags. "I thought we'd *never* arrive, William!" she said. "I couldn't have possibly survived one more bump! What terrible roads! We *never* had such horrid drives in New York!"

"And we never had such horrid people from New York," Henry said to Caroline.

Caroline giggled. She knew Henry was being naughty, but she couldn't help laughing. The woman was horrid.

"Mail!" the driver now called as he pulled the last sack from the top of the coach.

"Look, Caroline." Mother's voice turned Caroline's attention back to the stagecoach. "This stagecoach brings all the mail to Wisconsin from Boston and New York."

Mail! Caroline loved to hear Mother read the letters that Grandmother and Grandfather Tucker sent from Boston. Imagine that all those letters had to travel so far and over so many bumpy roads to get to Mother! It was no wonder they were so precious.

"I think we've seen enough, children," Mother said. "Come along now."

Reluctantly, Caroline followed Mother and Henry. She couldn't help but look back over her shoulder at the stagecoach. How exciting it must be to travel to new places! Maybe some day she too would travel on a stagecoach.

Caroline held Mother's hand tightly and squinted as she walked across the dusty road. All the horses and wagons going about their business in town had kicked up great clouds of dust. Caroline rubbed her stinging eyes as they passed the wagon maker's; the blacksmith's shop; a noisy, crowded tavern; and the shoemaker's. Finally they arrived at the general store.

"Come along, children," Mother said as she crossed the wooden plank sidewalk. Smiling and nodding, she excused herself as she made her way through the crowd of chattering men and women clustered outside sharing the news of the day.

Caroline followed right behind, watching the ground carefully. She had no choice but to walk through the dust in the street, but she didn't have to get too much dust on her shoes if she could help it. These shoes had belonged to Martha not long ago, and were worn and stained. Still, they didn't pinch her toes as her last pair had, and Caroline wanted them to stay as nice as they could until her feet outgrew them.

"Good day, Mrs. Carpenter. Good day, Mr. Carpenter," Mother said as they walked inside the store.

"And a good day to you, Mrs. Quiner!" a

man's voice boomed cheerfully.

The Carpenters lived two houses away from the Quiners, and they were good neighbors. Father and Mr. Carpenter had settled in Brookfield at the same time and helped clear each other's land. In the winter, Caroline could see the roof of the Carpenters' frame house from her bedroom window. Mrs. Carpenter often visited Mother when Mr. Carpenter and their son, Charles, went off hunting or fishing with Father, Joseph, and Henry. Martha always asked to go along on these trips, but Mother always said no. Caroline felt sorry for Martha, because she knew that Martha loved to be outdoors, away from chores like sewing and baking. But even more than that, Martha loved to be with Charlie Carpenter. Caroline didn't know why, because Charlie was always teasing Martha, and Martha usually did not like to be teased.

Since Father had died, Mr. Carpenter often helped Henry and Joseph with heavy chores. He and Charlie still took them along on fishing and hunting trips, and Mother still wouldn't let Martha go along.

Mother spoke with Mrs. Carpenter as Mr. Carpenter looked down at Caroline. The sleeves of his blue flannel shirt were pushed up to his elbows, and he rested his big, strong hands on his hips. "Well, hello there!" he said. Thick layers of his long brown hair fell in front of his dark eyes, but Caroline could still see the deep lines around his dark eyes crinkle when he smiled. "How is our little Brownbraid today?"

Mr. Carpenter had called Caroline "little Brownbraid" from the moment he first heard Father say it. His kind voice and eyes had always made Caroline feel happy, but whenever he was around now, she missed Father even more.

"Hello, Mr. Carpenter," Caroline answered quietly, hoping she wouldn't cry. Luckily, Henry came in just then with the sack of ashes.

Without saying a word, Mr. Carpenter grabbed one side of the sack while Henry lifted the other. Together, they swung it up onto the long pine-board counter. A little cloud of ash puffed up as the sack landed with a thud.

"Trading some ash, there, Ben?" Mr. Porter,

the grocer, looked up from his ledger. He was a tall man, so tall that the pots and kettles hanging from the ceiling nearly touched the top of his bald head. Tufts of gray hair hung over his ears, and his eyebrows looked like fluffy caterpillars. The buttons of his dark gray vest strained to hold in his round belly.

"Not today, Wills," Mr. Carpenter answered as he brushed ash off the front of his shirt. "Mr. Henry Quiner here brought this sack."

"Well, you've come at the right time. I'm about to send a shipment to the soap factory," Mr. Porter said. "Come, lad. Let's get this sack on the scale."

Henry, Mr. Carpenter, and the grocer disappeared into the back room. Mother was still deep in conversation with Mrs. Carpenter. Caroline wanted to explore the store, but she knew she shouldn't interrupt Mother. So she decided to slip away without asking.

Walking around to one side of the store, Caroline noticed that the wall in front of her looked just like the walls in their barn. Rakes and shovels and plows hung on it, as did hammers and knives, saws and hatchets. A big round barrel stuffed with brooms sat beside it.

Taking care not to bump into any of the hanging tools, Caroline walked past barrels and crates. She peered inside one of the barrels. Sticking out of the sawdust were hundreds of pointed tacks. Most of them were shiny, but a few had begun to turn rusty.

The cool, musty smell of the metal mixed with the scent of the sawdust in the crate beside it, and Caroline sneezed. Rubbing her nose, she looked into the crate, but she could see nothing in it but sawdust. On the side of the crate were four letters burned into the plain wood: A X E S.

Caroline knew two of the letters from her sampler, A and E. She knew the S meant that there was more than one. And she knew X from playing noughts and crosses with Henry.

I can read this, she thought. *Ay-ex. Silent E. Ayex. Ah-ex. Ahex. Axe. Axes!* She had almost stuck her hand in a crate of axes!

Caroline looked around to see if anyone had noticed, but no one was looking at her. Mother was now talking to the grocer. Caroline moved away from the crate of axes and went to the back of the store.

An assortment of rifles and muskets were stored there in a short, wide case. Beside the case, a small crate filled with lead balls stood next to a large keg that was tightly closed. Caroline knew that inside that keg was gunpowder.

Father used to let her and Martha watch him clean and load his gun. Joseph and Henry had often helped Father make bullets, and Caroline remembered Father's warning to her brothers: "Never leave this rifle unloaded, sons. A rifle must always be ready to shoot." Father would load the gun and hang it from two hooks above the door of their frame house. It was now Joseph's job to make certain the gun was always loaded and in its place above the door.

Next to the gun case, a set of shelves held china dishes. On each dish was a drawing of a shepherdess with a crook in her hand and two lambs next to her. The background was cream, and the drawing was blue. The edges of each plate were scalloped like petals on a flower.

Caroline thought the plates were the prettiest things she had ever seen. She wished she had a piece of china that was so pretty.

"Caroline!" came Mother's voice.

Caroline took one last look at the china dishes, then walked to the front of the store. Mother was standing at the counter, speaking with Mr. Porter. Henry was there, too, bouncing from foot to foot as he waited for Mother. His shirt was streaked with ashes.

Mother was saying, "I also need a small packet of tea, Mr. Porter, and some molasses, please."

Caroline watched as the grocer set the tea on the counter, and then pried open a big barrel of molasses. He lifted a ladle out of the barrel and carefully poured the thick, dark fluid into the empty jug Mother had given him. "Anything else, Mrs. Quiner?" he asked.

"I'd like one paper of sewing needles, and what's left of that bolt of dark blue calico," Mother answered.

"Are you certain you don't want to take wool this time of year, Mrs. Quiner?" the grocer said.

"Mrs. Carpenter just told me what she paid for wool," Mother answered tartly. "The cotton will serve my purpose for now."

"All right, then," Mr. Porter said. He looked up and down the three shelves that were filled with bolts of cloth until he found the material Mother wanted.

Caroline edged up to the counter so she could examine the shelves behind the grocer more closely. There were bolts of colored, dotted, and flowered cotton, wool, and silk. Buttons of all colors, sizes, and shapes were displayed, as well as thimbles and needles. Farther along the shelves Caroline spied slates and slate pencils, spelling books, and readers. The sweet smell of cinnamon sticks, nutmeg, cloves, and other spices mingled in the air. Right beside the spices were dainty soaps and candles, pickles and lemons, even hats and gloves. Caroline gazed at it all in wonder. How could anyone ever decide what to buy?

Ducking around to the other side of Mother, Caroline squeezed in beside Henry and peered at the top of the counter. One glass jar held tall, thin, red-and-white-striped sticks, while another held little round balls of assorted colors.

"Look, Henry!" Caroline whispered. "Candy!"

Sometimes Father brought home sweet sugar sticks, but since he'd gone, there had been no more candy.

"I wish I had a penny," said Henry longingly.

"That will be all. Thank you, Mr. Porter," Mother said.

"I'll credit you for the ashes, Mrs. Quiner, and I'll carry your balance until the next time you're in."

"That will be fine." Mother smiled at the grocer, picked up her basket of goods, and handed Henry the jug of molasses. "Please carry this, Henry," she said, turning for the door. "Come now, Caroline."

Caroline followed slowly, drinking in all

the sights one more time. The candy was tempting and some of the fabrics would make beautiful dresses, but Caroline decided that if she could buy anything she wanted in the store it would be a china shepherdess plate.

Frost

"The *Farmer's Almanac* says there's going to be a frost tonight," said Joseph at supper.

Henry snorted. "It feels like spring."

Henry was right. The sun had shone all day, making the autumn day warm and fresh. The children had worked in the garden, bringing in the last of the ripe tomatoes and beans, and Caroline had felt hot and itchy in the wool dress that Mother had insisted she wear. She was thankful the underground vegetables did not need to be picked yet.

"Do you think the *Farmer's Almanac* is correct?" said Mother.

Joseph shrugged. "It said it was supposed to rain for five days straight last month and it didn't."

In the middle of the night, Caroline dreamed that she was standing in the snow and couldn't move. She was so cold, and she knew all she had to do was take a step and she would be warm, but her legs were frozen stiff. She kept trying to move her legs.

"Don't kick me!" said Eliza.

Then Caroline was awake. She had only dreamed she was in the snow. But she was cold. A cold draft was moving around the room, and the covers were not warm enough to keep it out.

Caroline wanted to put another blanket on the bed, but she was too cold to move. She snuggled closer to Eliza and tried to get warm, but she couldn't. Her hands and feet were clenched, and she knew if she moved her legs at all, the cold air would get in.

Then she heard a door open and shut downstairs, and saw a light move across the window. She heard Henry say, "What's going on?"

Joseph got out of bed and went to the window. "It's Mother," he said. "She's in the garden."

Henry jumped out of bed and joined Joseph. "What on earth?"

"It's the frost, alright," said Joseph. "Just like the *Almanac* said. Mother must be getting the vegetables in. We have to go help her."

Mother in the garden in the middle of the night! Caroline jumped out of bed. She joined her brothers at the window. Mother was holding a torch and checking to see if the vegetables were freezing. Caroline knew that if vegetables froze before they were picked, they would rot.

"I'm going to help, too!" Caroline said, her teeth chattering.

"Get back to bed before you catch cold, Caroline," Joseph said sternly. "Henry and I will help Mother. I don't want you going out. You're too little."

Caroline knew that Joseph would not change his mind, and for once, she was glad he was so bossy. He and Henry would help Mother, and even though she wanted to do something to help, too, she knew she was too little to be of use in the garden at night. Still, it was maddening to be too young all the time. Why couldn't she be the oldest for a change?

Pickling Time

When Caroline woke up, she noticed something was different. What was it? Then she realized the light in the room had changed. Instead of the golden beams that usually poured in, there was a hazy muted light in the room.

"Oh, Eliza," Caroline said. "Come look!" The glass was covered with thick white frost. Caroline breathed on the glass to melt the frost and wiped the moisture away. Below them was a strange new landscape. A thick layer of ice covered the pine and maple trees, the roof of the barn, the henhouse and woodpile, and the entire garden. It was so different and so silent that it made Caroline feel very quiet.

Eliza pressed her nose against the glass. "Cold!" she wailed. Caroline laughed.

"Girls!" The urgent sound of Mother's voice sent the two sisters running down the stairs without bothering to change out of their night-gowns. At the bottom, Caroline stood stock still. Heaped in baskets, overflowing onto the floor, were dozens, even hundreds of vegetables: corn, peppers, yellow beans, green tomatoes, green pumpkins, and squash. Mother, Martha, and the boys had picked everything that was above ground in the garden last night. Grandma had helped, too. There were so many vegetables that there was barely room to walk.

A pail of new milk was sitting in the middle of the kitchen, as though Joseph had been too tired to set it in its usual place by the fire. The fire was small, as though Henry had not yet fed it new wood. There was no breakfast cooking.

Mother looked exhausted. There were dark circles under her eyes, and her hair was tumbling out of its usually neat bun. Caroline noticed that Mother's hands were crusted with dirt and her dress was muddy. Martha and the boys looked no better. They were all standing in the kitchen, swaying slightly, as though they were too tired even to sit down. Grandma was sitting in her rocking chair, her eyes closed.

Caroline felt ashamed for having slept in her warm bed all night. Despite what Joseph had said, she should have gone out to help. She was six after all, not just four like Eliza.

"Sit down, Mother," she said sternly. She pulled a chair out. Mother started to make a protest. "Sit down all of you," Caroline said. "I am making breakfast."

To her surprise, they all sat. Telling Eliza to mind Thomas, Caroline added two sticks of wood to the fire to get it going. She took the knife that Mother would not usually let her touch, and cut slice after thick slice of bread. Then she took the milk pail full of fresh creamy milk and poured it into the kettle. Joseph helped her lift the kettle and hook it on the cooking pole. She used the iron poker to push the cooking pole with the kettle to heat over the now-crackling fire.

Caroline then pulled a chair over to the dish cupboard and took down six bowls. She knew she was not tall enough to pour the milk into the bowls on the table, so she put the bowls on the ground next to the kettle. She put two slices of bread in each bowl, even though Mother generally put only one.

Now the milk was ready. She took the poker and pulled the cooking pole out of the fireplace. Wrapping the handle of the kettle in a towel as Mother always did, she lifted the kettle of milk off the pole. Slowly she poured some milk into each bowl, to cover the bread and make milk-toast.

Caroline placed each warm bowl on the table. She fetched spoons from the dish cupboard and sprinkled sugar in each bowl. Finally she sprinkled a little cinnamon in each—she had always thought that would taste delicious, although Mother never used cinnamon when she made milk-toast.

"Breakfast is ready," she said, and she sat down with her family.

After everyone had eaten breakfast, Mother said, "That was wonderful, Caroline. Thank you. Now we have more to do if we are to save these vegetables."

"What can we do with them?" asked Martha. "Most of them are unripe."

"Pickles," said Mother. "We will pickle them."

"I have heard of pickled onions and tomatoes," said Henry. "But I have never heard of pickled pumpkin and squash!"

Mother answered cheerfully, "And nor have I, but nothing ventured, nothing gained. Look at your sister. She has never made breakfast before, and yet, we just finished eating milk-toast, and with cinnamon." Mother's eyes twinkled at Caroline. "God gave us our minds to use them in new ways, not to do just what we have always done before. Now let's get to work!"

Mother's energy was contagious, and as Henry and Joseph continued to rake the garden for anything that had survived the frost, Grandma, Caroline, Martha, and Mother set to work with the vinegar and spices to make the strangest pickles any of them had ever heard of.

Happy Birthday

Winter had come to Brookfield.

The last potatoes, turnips, carrots, and beets had been pulled from the ground and stored safely in the root cellar beneath the kitchen. Jars of pickles and preserves lined the pantry shelves. But the barrels of dried fish were nearly empty, and the rafters that had once hung thick with dried meat when Father was alive were empty.

Joseph rushed through the kitchen door and slammed it shut against the swirling winds. He stamped his feet, and snow tumbled from his shoulders.

"Joseph, make certain that you clear up that floor," Mother said without even looking up from the shirt she was mending.

"Yes, ma'am," Joseph answered as he dropped his armful of logs into the wood box.

The flames in the hearth leaped and danced as Caroline sewed on her sampler. Her stomach grumbled with hunger, even though she and Martha had just put away the supper dishes. Tonight they had eaten only a little bit of fish and potatoes. Being so hungry made it hard to sew her sampler, she decided. The cloth felt stiffer, and the thread kept knotting.

Closing her eyes for a moment, Caroline tried to imagine the smell of hot, fresh bread, but all she could smell was the warm, smoky aroma of burning wood that always filled the room. Feeling even hungrier, she looked over at Grandma, who was knitting in the rocker beside her.

"Grandma," Caroline asked, "could you

please help me finish this stitch?"

"Why, of course, dear. Come. Sit up here," Grandma said, helping Caroline onto her lap.

Grandma examined Caroline's sampler and whispered into her ear, "Your work is lovely." She covered Caroline's hands with her own, and together they began pulling the needle through the stiff cloth while Caroline watched closely.

"All finished!" Henry shouted. He jumped up from the floor and showed the handful of shavings he had made to Mother. "There's enough to stoke the fire come morning. All right if we play checkers now?"

Mother nodded. "Yes, you may play checkers."

Henry dropped the shavings in the tinderbox by the hearth, and Joseph pulled out their homemade checkerboard and corncob checkers. Caroline loved watching her brothers play checkers. They always sat on the floor in front of the fire and played quietly until Henry jumped one of Joseph's checkers. Scooping up the checker he'd just jumped, Henry would shout, "Whoop! Beat you at that one, Joseph!"

and slam it on the floor next to his side of the board. Henry's "Whoop!" always made Caroline want to laugh out loud. Even Mother smiled as she tried to shush Henry.

The fire hissed and popped, and tree branches tapped at the windowpanes as Mother, Caroline, and Martha sewed. Then Mother began to sing:

"Green grows the laurel, and so does
the rue;
So woeful my love, at the parting
with you.
But by our next meeting our love
we'll renew;
We'll change the green laurel to the
orange and blue."

Caroline knew each word of the song by heart, because Mother had been singing it ever since Father had gone away on his schooner. Sometimes Caroline wondered what a laurel and a rue were and how the green laurel could change to orange and blue.

Caroline remembered how Father used to wait every evening until Mother began sewing. Even before Mother was settled in her rocker, Father would whisk Caroline and Martha up onto his lap and say, "Sing now, Charlotte! We've all waited too long!" Mother's singing would fill the room, and Father would close his eyes and listen. It wasn't until she finished the last note that he'd look up at the rafters and whisper, "Heavenly! Like listening to the angels, your mother when she sings!"

"Whoop! Beat you at that one, Joseph!" Henry shouted gleefully.

Mother stopped singing and looked sternly at Henry. "Henry," she said, "he who knows how to keep silent knows a great deal."

"Yes, Mother." Henry tried to hide the grin on his face as Caroline pressed her hands to her mouth to stifle her own giggles.

"Could you sing another song now, Mother? A faster one?" Martha pleaded. Martha didn't like slow songs. She always wanted to dance, and she liked it best when Mother's singing was bright and lively.

"What song would you like?" Mother asked.

"Polly-wolly-doodle!" Martha cried.

Mother smiled, her eyes crinkling up at the corners. Setting the gray shirt she was mending on her lap, she began clapping and singing:

"Oh, I went down south for to see my Sal,
Sing polly-wolly-doodle all the day;
My Sally was a spunky gal,
Sing polly-wolly-doodle all the day.
Farewell, farewell, farewell, my fairy fay,
For I'm off to Louisiana
For to see my Susy Anna,
Singing polly-wolly-doodle all the day."

Skirt and braids swinging back and forth, Martha clapped and danced in front of the hearth. Caroline tied up the last strand of thread on her sampler and jumped down from Grandma's lap to join Martha. Henry and Joseph pushed the checkerboard aside, and they all joined hands and spun around until they got dizzy.

"That's enough, children," Mother said after she stopped singing. "I must work on Mrs. Stoddard's dress now," she said. Mrs. Stoddard lived in one of the grandest houses in Brookfield, and Caroline thought the dresses that Mother made for her were the most beautiful clothes in the world.

Mother spread long layers of dark green, crinkly material over the sewing table. It flowed off the table all the way to the floor. It was so exquisite, it hardly seemed possible it could be a dress.

"Where did such pretty material come from, Mother?" Caroline asked.

"Mrs. Stoddard had it sent from back East," Mother replied. Her nimble fingers pushed the needle and thread back and forth through the material so quickly that Caroline could barely follow them. No one could sew faster or better than Mother, Caroline thought proudly. Before she met Father, Mother had her own dress shop in Boston. Soon after Father was lost, Mother began making dresses and shirts again.

"When will Mrs. Stoddard wear such a pretty dress?" Martha asked.

"For Christmas," Mother said.

Caroline and Martha looked at each other, their eyes glowing. "Christmas!" Martha said. "How soon until Christmas?"

"Soon." Mother smiled. "A few weeks after Caroline's birthday."

Caroline caught her breath. "When is my birthday, Mother?"

"Four more days, Caroline."

"But I thought I didn't have a birthday," Caroline said hesitantly.

Mother looked up abruptly from the dark-green cloth. "Why, of course you do. Whatever makes you think that you do not?" she asked.

Caroline had often wondered how she had turned six without a birthday, but she had never asked Mother. "We didn't celebrate Caroline's birthday last year, Mother," Martha said quietly. "We had just heard the news about Father."

Mother's face fell, and Caroline wished that Martha had never said those words. All of a sudden Caroline remembered Mother saying, "Father will be home any day now, children. As soon as the schooner comes back to port." But instead, Uncle Elisha, Aunt Margaret, and Grandma had arrived from the big city of Milwaukee. Mother left the house to greet them as Caroline, her brothers, and Martha watched from the window in the parlor.

Closing her eyes tightly, Caroline tried to forget seeing Uncle Elisha help Grandma and Aunt Margaret out of the wagon. They were all dressed in black. Aunt Margaret clutched a white handkerchief, and she wiped away the tears that streamed down her cheeks. Uncle Elisha looked at the ground and scuffed the toe of his black boot in the dirt. When he finally looked up, Caroline saw that his eyes were red and puffy. Grandma's face was hidden by a long black veil, and Uncle Elisha had his arm tucked solidly beneath hers. "Something is wrong," Joseph had said. No one spoke or moved. They all just watched as Mother buried her face in her hands, and Aunt Margaret hugged her. Grandma, Uncle Elisha, and Aunt

Margaret had come that day to tell them that Father's schooner had been lost in a terrible storm. Uncle Elisha and Aunt Margaret stayed in the frame house for many, many days, until Mother felt better, and Grandma had lived with them ever since. Father had never returned.

"I remember now," Mother said. Kneeling down in front of Caroline, Mother looked into her eyes. "We didn't celebrate your birthday last year because we were all too sad for a celebration. But this year we aren't sad, Caroline. This year you will have your birthday."

Suddenly Caroline was in a terrible hurry to get to bed so that she could help the days go by faster. Running up the stairs ahead of Martha, she could think of nothing else. Her birthday! All hers! Hardly noticing the chill in the room, she pulled on her nightgown, tucked her hair inside her cap, and climbed in under the covers. Only four more days!

It seemed to Caroline that the next three days lasted a whole week. Never had chores seemed so endless. Never had time passed so slowly. But finally her birthday arrived. It was still dark when Caroline opened her eyes on the fourth day. She crept out of bed and dressed so quietly she didn't wake anyone. She brushed her hair until it shone and tiptoed downstairs with her blue ribbon. Grandma and Mother were just beginning to prepare breakfast.

"My goodness, Caroline!" Mother exclaimed. "It is very early for you to be up!"

"Yes, Mother," Caroline answered shyly. She hoped it was still her birthday and that she hadn't miscounted.

"Wash your hands and face. You can use the fresh water in that bucket over there."

Mother nodded toward the kitchen door, and Caroline knelt down and scooped the cold water into her hands. She took care not to soak the ends of her sleeves. She was seven years old now and a seven-year-old could not be careless about such things.

The juicy smell of frying fat began to fill the kitchen. "Are you making hotcakes, Mother?" Caroline asked hopefully.

"Why, of course. Today we're celebrating your birthday!" Mother smiled. "Come, let's braid your hair and get you ready for your special day."

Caroline held her blue ribbon out to Grandma, but Mother said quickly, "I'll braid your hair today, Caroline. Will you please finish stirring this, Mother Quiner?" Handing the bowl and spoon to Grandma, Mother sat on a chair behind Caroline and began twisting and pulling her hair into one long brown braid. As Mother's nimble fingers neared the bottom of her braid, Caroline handed her the blue ribbon.

"Oh, Caroline," Mother said, "you cannot wear such an old ribbon on your birthday! She spun Caroline around. Lying in Mother's hand was a brand-new ribbon made of the same soft cloth as Mrs. Stoddard's dress.

"Oh, Mother." Caroline could barely speak. "It's so beautiful."

"Happy birthday!" Mother laughed and tied the ribbon in a bow around the bottom of Caroline's braid.

But that was not all. Mother reached inside her apron pocket and pulled out a small bundle that was wrapped in a swatch of tan cloth. Caroline gently unfolded the cloth. Smiling up at her was a cheery rag doll. Black button eyes winked in the early-morning light, and the black yarn doll's braid reached all the way to the waist of her plaid dress. Caroline lovingly cradled the doll and touched her dark-green bow, which perfectly matched Caroline's brand-new bow.

"My very own doll! I shall call her Abigail!"

"Grandma helped make Abigail," Mother said. "You must thank her, also."

Caroline hurried to hug Grandma as Mother said, "And now I must wake your brothers and sisters so that we can all celebrate together."

Caroline took care of her doll while the rest of the family got up. Soon everyone was gathered around the table in the warm, sunny kitchen, feasting on hotcakes and dried apples. They had never had such a merry breakfast! No one even noticed that the hotcakes were made of cornmeal, or that there was no butter or syrup to spread on them.

Caroline held Abigail tightly with one hand and kept reaching behind her back with the other. She wanted to be certain that her precious bow was still safely wrapped around her braid. Who could ever have thought of *two* presents for a birthday?

The Christmas Stranger

Mother picked up an empty jug and basket lying on the kitchen floor. "It's time to go, Caroline," she said.

There was no more flour in the bin. Mother had used up the last of it, and now there was none left for her to make her special Christmas bread for tomorrow. Joseph had gone to town to trade some rabbit pelts for a few cups of flour, but Mr. Leavenworth did not need any rabbit pelts. He had enough already, he said. If Father had been alive, he would have been able to trade some beaver or even a bear pelt for the flour. But Father was not alive, and now there would be no Christmas bread.

"Will we starve to death?" asked Caroline.

"Of course not, child!" exclaimed Mother. "We have plenty of potatoes and onions and pickled tomatoes. We will be just fine."

Potatoes and onions and tomatoes. That is all they had now to eat—every dinner and every supper, and maybe every breakfast, too, now that there was no flour. Onions and potatoes and tomatoes, tomatoes and potatoes and onions, potatoes and tomatoes and onions. Whichever way you said it, it was still the same. Succotash. Caroline knew she should feel grateful for even that, but she did not. She wanted Christmas bread.

The day inched along, filled with chores and the sound of the blowing wind, which rattled the panes and shook the house. Finally it was time for bed. Mother listened as the children said their prayers:

"Now I lay me down to sleep,
I pray the Lord my soul to keep.

If I should die before I wake,
I pray the Lord my soul to take.
And please bless Father and keep him
in heaven with You forever. Amen."

Mother went downstairs. Outside the wind howled and the branches tip-tapped against the glass windows. Caroline could not sleep. She remembered the musty smoke from Father's pipe that had wandered upstairs every night. She remembered his big laugh and how he used to tease Mother and make her smile. She did not want to believe he was gone forever. And if Father were still here, they would have plenty to eat, and Mother would not look so worried. And they would have Christmas bread.

Caroline thought about their last Christmas with Father. The year before he went away, Father had carved little wooden dolls for his girls, and the checkerboard for the boys. Mother had cooked a meal that was so enormous, there had hardly been any room left on the table for dishes or cups. There was a goose full of fruit stuffing, turkey and ham, squash, onions, and potatoes, baked apples, plum pudding, and a mince pie for dessert. Father had declared Mother's Christmas dinner a feast fit for a king, and had chuckled and told stories until even the fire in the hearth began to sputter and fall asleep. Caroline wished that Christmas could be that happy again. If Father were still here, he'd get Mother some flour for Christmas; Caroline just knew it.

The next thing Caroline knew, it was morning, and she was all alone in the bed. She pushed the curtain back. No Henry or Joseph. She had slept later than anyone else; no one had woken her up. Slowly she got dressed. She brushed her hair. She braided it. She made the bed. She made Henry and Joseph's bed. She did not want to go downstairs and eat succotash. She did not want to wish Father were here. The fact that it was Christmas only made her ache for him hurt worse.

Finally there was nothing more to do. She had to go downstairs. She went through the opening in the attic floor. She slowly put each foot down on the next step. Five more steps, four more, three more, two, one. She was in the kitchen.

"Merry Christmas, sleepyhead!" everyone shouted. Caroline's eyes grew wide. On Mother's special bread plate was a loaf of her special braided, golden-brown Christmas bread.

"Sit down so we can eat!" said Henry.

"And find out how Mother made the bread," added Martha.

Caroline slipped into her chair, staring at the bread. Mother cut thick slices of the good, warm bread, and everyone heaped honey on them. As they ate, Mother told the story.

"Last night I was sitting in my rocking chair, feeling like it could not be Christmas without Christmas bread. I was even thinking about how I might use the corn husks to make some sort of cornmeal for the bread, when there was a knocking at the door. I got the rifle down, because I could not imagine who could be stopping by at such a late hour. I told whoever it was to come in. It was a man I had never seen. He was bundled in a heavy fur coat and wearing a fur cap.

"He tipped his cap and set down a sack inside the door. He said, 'Merry Christmas to you and your young'uns from a friend,' and then he was gone before I could find out why he was here or even what his name was.

"And what do you think was in the sack?" asked Mother.

"Candy!" said Eliza.

"Money!" said Henry.

"Flour," said Caroline, taking a big bite of the satisfying bread.

"Caroline is correct, and you should all have guessed that, for how could I have made this bread without flour?" said Mother.

"But why did he give us flour?" asked Henry.

Mother was silent. "I don't know," she said at last.

"I can only think it was the good Lord's work," Grandma said thoughtfully.

Joseph had been squirming in his chair. "Did he have on a raccoon cap, Mother, with two raccoon tails hanging down?"

"Why, yes, he did," Mother said wonderingly.

"And did he have a deep scar across his cheek?"

Mother's eyes went wide. "Yes."

"And did he smell a little funny, like a bear, maybe, or some kind of animal?"

"It isn't polite to discuss people's smells, Joseph," said Mother sternly. Then she smiled. "But now that you mention it, yes, he did."

"I know who it is!" cried Joseph triumphantly. "I saw him at the mill yesterday when I tried to trade those rabbit pelts for some flour. He was standing behind me, waiting his turn to trade his pelts. He had so many: bear, beaver, raccoon, even wolf. I think he was a trapper, and that's why he smelled so—"

"Joseph," warned Mother.

"Well, anyway," continued Joseph, "he must have overheard me telling Mr. Leavenworth that we had no flour left and seen that Mr. Leavenworth would not take my pelts. I seem to remember he nodded to me as I left."

Mother sat back. Finally she said, "I don't

like taking charity, but we surely do need the flour. This man, whoever he was, has given us a great gift."

"Flour?" said Caroline.

"Yes, but even more, the gift of kindness, and that is a gift you should always give and always accept."

Soon the talk turned to other things, like how the hens seemed to know it was Christmas and had laid three eggs that morning instead of two. Caroline looked at the bread on her plate. She took a big bite. Kindness tasted delicious.

Wagon Pie

Bent over a slate scribbled with numbers, Martha rested her chin in her hand and sighed heavily. Caroline, too, felt the dullness of the long winter day spreading over the frame house like a heavy gray blanket. And the hungry tightness in her stomach didn't help matters.

"When will Henry and Joseph be home, Mother?" Martha asked. Henry and Joseph had started school right after the new year. Every morning they trudged three miles to the schoolhouse through drifts of blowing snow.

"At suppertime, as they are every day,"

Mother answered. "Why do you ask?"

"Oh, I just hoped they might come home early today," Martha said. She raised her head and looked at Mother, her big eyes shining. "A fresh snow fell last night, and I want to play fox and geese!"

"It's time for your lessons now, Martha, not for playing. Sit up straight and begin your sums. You can return to your readings later."

Caroline did not miss Joseph very much, who spent most days away from home hunting anyway. But she missed Henry, and thought it was unfair that she could not go to school, too. Henry had a new reader that Grandma Tucker had sent him from Boston with all kinds of printed stories and poems that he had not yet read. Caroline had only a yellowed sheet of handwritten Bible verses that she already knew by heart.

"Sit up straight, Caroline, and copy the fourth verse. Your handwriting is still not as neat as it should be," said Mother. The sheet had belonged to Mother first. Grandma Tucker had written it out for Mother when she was a little girl to teach her how to read and write. It was hard to imagine Mother as a little girl.

"Yes, Mother," said Caroline gloomily.

Pride goeth before destruction, and a haughty spirit before a fall, Caroline scratched on her slate. Her slate pencil was not sharp enough, and she did not have as much room at the table to write as she needed. She liked to make her letters big and round, and to do that she needed a lot of space.

"Ouch!" said Martha, rubbing her arm. "Stop poking me with your elbow."

"I am not poking you. You are too close to me," Caroline snapped back.

"Girls," said Mother. "Be quiet. Eliza and Thomas are sleeping. Move over to give your sister more room, Martha."

Both girls fell silent. Caroline scratched on, the tip of her tongue sticking out with the effort of making the *s* in *goes*. If she was not careful, she sometimes wrote it backward. Then Martha started kicking the table leg. It made the tabletop jiggle, and the bottom of Caroline's *s* wobbled all over the slate.

"Stop that, Martha!" cried Caroline.

"I'm not doing anything," said Martha innocently.

"Mother, Martha is kicking the table so that I will make mistakes."

"Martha, stop kicking the table," Mother said immediately. "And Caroline, don't tattle. It is a very unattractive quality."

Caroline did not say anything, but itched to slap Martha, and her hand twitched a little. Mother saw.

"Girls, you should be ashamed of yourselves," she said in a voice that they rarely heard her use. It was her disappointed voice. They looked up at her, already sorry for how they had behaved. "Do you know how lucky you are to be able to sit in a warm house and study all day? Do you know there are children who must work in factories all day who never learn to read and write? And that there are children who are so poor and hungry that, even if they had a teacher, they would not have the energy to learn? Now stop your squabbling and behave like good girls."

Mother returned to her mending. Martha bent over her work, her arms and legs still. Caroline felt ashamed. She had been unkind to her sister, and had tattled. She had taken for granted things that some children did not have and never would have. Worst of all, she had disappointed Mother. She vowed right then to be not just a good little girl but to be the best little girl there ever was and make Mother proud of her. A warm glow filled her as she thought how well behaved she would be and how much Mother would love her—even if it was true that Martha had kicked her.

Caroline looked back at her verses and had just begun to copy out a new verse when the door swung open and Joseph and Henry blew in from the cold.

"Goodness glory!" Mother exclaimed. "Whatever are you boys doing home so early?"

Joseph unwrapped his scarf from around his neck and said breathlessly, "Everyone went home early today, Mother."

"After recess, Danny McCarthy brought a huge snowball back into the schoolhouse and left it on the schoolmaster's chair," Henry jumped in, his eyes twinkling.

Caroline and Martha held their breath, waiting to hear what happened next. Joseph continued. "Mr. Henderson didn't notice and sat down right in the middle of a cold, wet pile of slush."

Henry burst out laughing. "You should have seen it, Mother!" he roared. "I never saw anybody jump so high! Why, he practically hit the rafters!"

Caroline wanted to laugh, too, but then she remembered, and made her face stern. It was not nice to tease the schoolmaster. "That Daniel McCarthy has been nothing but trouble since he and his folks arrived in Brookfield. I hope the schoolmaster punished him for his disrespect!" said Mother.

"He tried, Mother," Joseph answered, "but Danny ran out of the school before he could do anything."

"He was so angry, though, that he went right after Danny, without stopping to put on his coat or say anything to us." Henry paused. "He never came back, and after a while, we figured that meant we had been given an early dismissal."

Caroline watched Mother's eyes dance. She thought she saw the corners of Mother's mouth twitch.

"Very well, boys. You may finish your lessons with your sisters."

Martha burst out, "Oh, Mother, I know I've been bad today, but please can we all go out and play fox and geese?"

"Have you finished your sums, Martha?" Mother asked.

"Almost all of them, Mother. I can finish the others tomorrow. I promise I will." Clasping her hands together, Martha pleaded, "Please, may we go outside?"

"Oh, yes, please, Mother!" said Henry and Joseph.

Caroline almost chimed in with Martha and her brothers, but then she remembered. She would be kind and well behaved and not beg to do something fun, even if it meant she had to do her lesson all afternoon. She hoped Mother noticed how good she was being.

Mother looked at the eager faces of Martha, Henry, and Joseph and said, "Well, just this once." They cheered, and Martha jumped up from the table to put on her coat, hat, and mittens.

"But, Caroline," continued Mother, "you are very quiet. Would you rather stay indoors? Are you feeling ill?"

Caroline did not know what to do. Mother had not seen how good she was being. Instead, Mother thought she was ill. If she stayed indoors, Mother would give her a dose of bitter-tasting medicine when she wasn't even sick. She was confused.

Then a thought came to her. If Mother thought she were ill, she would worry about Caroline. And if Mother thought she were ill when she was not, that was almost like lying. In fact, that was lying. And making Mother worry when she did not have to and lying were not good things. Of that Caroline was sure.

Her choice was clear. By going outside she would not worry Mother and she would not be lying.

"Oh, no, Mother, I want to go!" Caroline shouted, jumping up for joy.

As soon as they were all bundled up, the children ran into the yard. The snow sparkled in the sunlight, and the wind had all but disappeared.

"Let's make the circle fast!" Joseph shouted.

Together they began to stamp the newly fallen snow into a gigantic circle. Joseph and Henry pushed their way through knee-deep drifts of ice and snow, while Caroline and Martha stomped behind them until the snow was packed firmly on the ground.

As soon as the outside circle was done, Henry and Joseph trudged across its thick center four times, cutting the circle into eight equal wedges. Then they ran to the point where all the trails met and stomped out a small circle right in the center.

"All ready!" Henry bellowed. He and Joseph stood back to admire their work, and Caroline and Martha ran down a snow trail and met them in the middle of the circle.

"I think it looks just like a wagon wheel," Joseph said.

"Reminds me of one of Mother's pies!" Henry said. "Eight slices of pie!"

"A wagon pie!" Caroline cried.

Joseph laughed. "Now, let's pick a fox."

"You be the fox this time, Caroline," Henry said, his words turning into wisps of steam.

They stood in the circle facing one another. Martha, Joseph, and Henry held out mittened fists. Caroline clapped her mittens together and counted around the circle of hands, hitting a different fist with every word she spoke.

"Wire, briar, limber lock,
Three geese in a flock
One flew east, one flew west,
One flew over the cuckoo's nest.
O-U-T . . . OUT!"

As soon as Caroline said "Out," Henry, Joseph, and Martha each flew down a different trail of the wagon pie as fast as they could.

Caroline had to chase them and tag one of them before they returned to the inner circle or she would have to be the fox again. She ran after Joseph.

Henry arrived at the inner circle first. "Home free!" he called.

"Home free!" Martha called as she arrived next.

Caroline lunged after her oldest brother as he ran toward the inner circle and grabbed the bottom corner of his jacket. She slipped forward and fell into a powdery bank of snow. Joseph tumbled with a big *crunch!* right next to Caroline.

"Good catch!" he said, laughing. Caroline decided she liked him after all, even if he wasn't usually as merry as Henry.

Laughing and running as fast as they could, Henry and Martha scampered down a trail of the wagon pie and pulled Joseph and Caroline up from their chilly nest of snow. Martha brushed chunks of snow and ice from Caroline's scarf, shawl, and braid, and took hold of her mittened hand. Together they skipped and slid back to the center circle, where Joseph now called out the fox's rhyme so loudly that it echoed across all the snow-covered trees.

Pink wisps of clouds hung from the sky as the sun dropped below the pine trees. Caroline and Martha and Henry and Joseph chased each other up and down the wagon-pie trails until the light faded, and Mother called them inside for supper.

Cakes and Candlesticks

Caroline tapped her feet restlessly on the floor. Laying her sampler on the sewing table, she went to the window and looked outside. Raindrops pelted the windowpanes and slipped to the bottom of the glass. The sky was as dark as twilight, and it wasn't even dinnertime yet. Caroline knew it would be ages before her brothers came home.

"Do you think that spring will ever come, Grandma?" she asked, her breath making little patches of fog on the cold glass.

"Of course it will," Grandma answered.

"Why, it's April. Spring is already here."

Martha looked up from her knitting. "But if spring's here, Grandma," she said, "where is the sunshine? When is it ever going to be warm enough to go outside? I'm so tired of being inside all the time!"

"Patience, Martha," Grandma said. "I have never heard of a year in which spring did not come." Caroline thought about what it would be like to have winter but no spring. Would it just be summer one day? Or if spring never came did that mean summer couldn't come either?

"What's all this I hear about spring?"

Caroline turned away from the window and looked closely at Mother as she entered the room. Caroline wondered where she had been and why her eyes looked so red. Every morning after chores, Mother was busy working at the sewing table. But this morning when Caroline and Martha came downstairs after straightening their room, Mother hadn't been at the table. She hadn't even been in the room.

"The girls were just saying how much they'd

like to be outside, Charlotte," Grandma answered. "And I can't blame them. I'm eager for spring to bring warmer weather myself."

Mother stood beside Caroline and looked out at all the dreariness. "It does seem as though it's been either snowing or raining forever," she said. "I think we need a celebration!"

"A celebration!" Martha dropped her knitting and clapped. "What will we celebrate, Mother?"

Mother's eyes were suddenly as bright as her voice. "We'll celebrate springtime. We'll welcome the spring."

"Welcome spring!" Eliza repeated.

Mother was now surrounded by her three girls. "How will we celebrate, Mother?" Martha asked.

"We'll make a treat. Something simple but special." Mother said cheerfully. She lifted Eliza into her arms and looked down at Martha's and Caroline's expectant faces. "Come along. Let's see what we can find in the pantry."

In no time at all, Mother had placed two

eggs, a spoonful of salt, and a small bowl of flour on the table. "We can make some delightful cakes with this," she decided. "Martha, while I get the grease melting, please crack the eggs in here and beat them until they are light and fluffy." Handing a big bowl to Martha, Mother crossed to the stove while Caroline and Eliza watched Martha beat the eggs.

Mother picked up a tub full of lard, scooped a few thick spoonfuls into a deep pan, and placed it on the stove in front of the simmering pot of stew. Then she went back to the table to check on Martha's egg mixture.

"They look perfectly fluffy, Martha." Mother nodded her approval and reached for the bowl of flour.

Scooping up a small amount in a ladle, Mother handed the flour to Caroline and said, "It's your turn, Caroline. While I stir, please sprinkle this slowly over the batter."

Caroline carefully dusted the top of the eggs with the flour while Mother kept mixing, adding more flour until the batter was too stiff to beat.

Then Mother pushed the dough together until it formed a round ball and kneaded it quickly. She tossed a sprinkling of flour over the top of the table, pinched little pieces from the big ball of dough, and handed one each to Caroline, Martha, and Eliza.

Picking up a bit of dough and showing them how, Mother said, "Roll the piece of dough between your palms like this until it forms a little ball. Then set the ball on the table."

Each girl did as she was told, and Mother flattened their dough balls until they were just thin enough not to tear when she slowly peeled each one up from the table.

"Time to check the fat," she said. The hot lard was sputtering and popping as Mother peered into the pan. It was time to fry the cakes. She dropped the flattened balls in one by one as Caroline and Martha stood on tiptoe looking into the pan but keeping a safe distance from the bubbling fat.

Each little cake was immediately surrounded by tiny bubbles as it felt into the pool of hot fat. The cakes sizzled and fried and swelled into big doughy puffs that floated to the surface of the pan. Within a minute or two, every cake had flipped over in the hot fat and turned a golden brown.

"They look so lovely, Mother!" Martha exclaimed.

Mother smiled. "Now hurry and set the table for dinner. We can't waste any time, or these cakes will get too cool and taste much less delicious!"

Caroline and Martha hurried to gather plates and cups from the dish dresser. Mother carefully lifted each cake out of the hot lard with a long-handled spoon, then set it on a flat tin that was covered with a clean rag. As she turned away from the stove and walked to the table to set the tin of cakes down, Eliza called out, "I want to see, too!"

Mother whirled around just as Eliza reached up to grab the handle of the pan on the stove. The tin banged down on the table as Mother dropped the cakes. "No!" Mother screamed, and ran toward Eliza. "Stop, Eliza!"

Grandma dropped her needlework and rushed toward the stove when she heard Mother scream. Eliza stopped her hand in midair. Her eyes filled with tears and her lip began to quiver. "I'm . . . I'm sorry," she cried as Mother gathered her up and carried her away from the hot stove.

"My little Eliza," Mother admonished as she pulled her close and stroked her soft blond curls. "You must never, never go near the stove again. Never!"

"But I didn't get to see," Eliza hiccupped between sobs.

Setting Eliza back down on the floor, Mother held her arms firmly and looked into her teary blue eyes. "Goodness sakes, Eliza, you scared the daylights out of me! I was certain you'd burn yourself worse than your father did years ago!" Mother hugged her once more. "Now go sit with Grandma while I help your sisters get dinner on the table."

Caroline looked at Martha, and she could tell from the surprise in her big sister's eyes that she was just as shocked that Mother had mentioned father. Mother rarely spoke about Father, and when she did it was only to answer one of the children's questions.

After setting the plates on the table, Martha asked Mother hesitantly, "Would you tell us the story of the candlesticks?"

"Please, Mother," added Caroline. "We haven't heard that story since Father went away."

Mother smiled but she couldn't hide the sadness in her eyes as she said, "Let's all sit down to dinner now. I will tell you the candlestick story."

After every bowl had been filled with the steaming stew, corn bread had been passed around the table, and grace had been said, Mother began her story.

"When your father and I decided to be married we sent notice to my folks in Boston and asked that they come to New Haven for the wedding. After weeks of waiting for a reply, we learned that none of my relatives would be able to come, and your father and I agreed that we should be married without delay. But Father needed a few more days to complete a gift he was making for me."

"Father was a silversmith then, wasn't he?" Martha asked.

"Yes, Martha. Father heated silver until it melted. He'd then transfer it from the furnace to a big block of steel, where he would pound it into a teapot, a porringer, or a serving piece. Sometimes the silver wasn't yet hot enough to shape, so Father had to carry it back to the furnace and heat it more."

"Father's job was very dangerous, so I expected a few mishaps now and then. What I feared most was that he'd be badly burned by the hot silver."

"Did you tell him so?" Caroline asked.

"I certainly did, Caroline. Father would laugh and say, 'Wouldn't be any fun if'n I were to worry 'bout such things, Charlotte! I'm careful as I need be, and 'til I have reason, I'll not borrow trouble by thinking such things!' "

"Tell us about the candlesticks, Mother!" Martha prompted.

"If I keep telling stories, I'll never get a

warm bite of stew," Mother teased. "Well, our wedding day dawned a bright, cold day in late March. I was at the Reverend's early, and I waited and waited for Father to arrive for the wedding, but he never did. Here I'd left home, family, dress shop, and all for Henry Quiner, and he hadn't even bothered to come to the Reverend Cushman's and take our vows."

"What did you do?" Martha and Caroline called out together.

"I told the Reverend that I needed to wait right there in his parlor. I was certain that your father would come. The Reverend agreed, and there I sat, waiting for Father. It was long after dark when we both finally agreed that Father would probably not come."

"Oh, Mother!" Martha cried. "Where was Father?"

"I didn't know. I told the Reverend I would never speak to Henry again."

"This is the part when Father comes back!" Caroline clapped her hands.

Her smile now joyful, Mother finished the story. "That very moment, I opened the door to leave. There was your father, wearing a fine black jacket and a starched white shirt. His hair and beard were combed more neatly than I had ever seen. He didn't smile at me; he didn't beg for my forgiveness. He simply said, 'Unwrap your gift this minute, Charlotte, so we can have the Reverend marry us before the sunrise ends our wedding day.' "

"What did you do?" Caroline begged Mother to finish the story.

"I looked right at your father and I said, 'I will open a wedding gift only after there's been a proper wedding, Henry Quiner.' Father reached for my hand, and it was then that I discovered the bandages that covered his fingers, hand, and arm. 'Goodness glory, Henry!' I cried. 'Whatever happened to you?' Father took my arm in his and said, 'Hush, now, Charlotte. We'll have a whole lifetime for me to tell the story.' "

Tears were shining in Mother's eyes. "The Reverend married us that very moment."

"And the candlesticks?" Martha asked softly.

"They were the last silver pieces that Father

ever made. The morning of our wedding day he was finishing them, and he accidentally spilled some of the hot metal on his hand and arm. Father was so badly burned that it took the doctor hours to apply salve and bandages. The burns took months to heal, and his hand remained badly scarred. Father decided he'd give trading a try." Mother blinked the tears away as she finished her story. "I've treasured those candlesticks for fifteen years now, girls." Mother smiled. "I shall treasure them until the day I die."

"Why, Charlotte," Grandma exclaimed, "today's your anniversary!"

"Yes, Mother Quiner," Mother said softly.

"We must have the candlesticks on the table while we eat our cakes," Grandma said. "This is a celebration day, after all."

"Oh please, Mother, please!" Caroline and Martha echoed.

Mother went to get the candlesticks, and by the time she returned, Grandma, Caroline, and Martha had cleared the dinner dishes. Only the tray of cakes was left on the table. Mother set the candlesticks down on either side.

"Oh, Mother," Caroline whispered, "they're so beautiful."

Each candlestick was a long, thin silver pillar. The top of the candlestick was flattened and slightly wider than the pillar, which descended to the table in flat, wide steps. Around each pillar, Father had fashioned a delicate floral design.

Mother lovingly pressed a candle into each candlestick. Then she lit the end of a bit of tinder from a flame in the hearth and set the candles aglow.

"Now we have a real celebration." Mother looked from her candlesticks to her daughters.

In the soft glow of candlelight, she served the cakes all around the table. They were still warm and crunchy. Caroline bit into hers, and she thought that it tasted very much like a bubble might taste: light and airy and quick to disappear. Silently, she savored every bite.

Church

The last lumps of snow finally melted. Tender blades of grass poked up from the cool dark soil, and the trees clothed themselves in tight buds and pale green leaves.

"We're going to church tomorrow," Mother said one day. She pulled the girls' church dresses from the chest and laid them on her bed. Martha was going to wear a new dress because she had outgrown her old one. It was a beautiful sky blue, and it had a crisp white collar and little yellow flowers. Mother had made it for her over the winter. Caroline had also outgrown her dress, but she did not get a new dress to wear. She was going to wear Martha's old dress. It had a torn collar, and its plain yellow material had faded. Mother had cleaned and ironed it, and repaired the collar, but it still looked like Martha's old dress. Caroline bit her lip and tried not to mind, but she could not help herself. It was not fair that Martha always had a new dress to wear and she always had to wear Martha's hand-me-downs. Martha didn't even care about dresses.

That night, the girls took baths, and so did the boys. They went to bed. Martha chattered about who they would see in church the next day.

"Maybe Mrs. Stoddard will be there, and the Ewings," she said. "And the Carpenters, of course."

Caroline knew she meant Charlie Carpenter, but she did not say anything. She just turned over on her side and stared at the wall. She was so mad about the dress, she just could not talk to Martha. But Martha did not notice and kept chattering away. Eventually she fell asleep, but

Caroline was awake long into the night, thinking mean thoughts that made her throat tight and her stomach hurt.

The next morning was no better. Caroline put on the old dress. It fit perfectly. She would have to wear it all spring and all summer. She could just feel the stains in it, even if she could not see them.

Martha put on her beautiful blue dress.

"Button me up, Caroline," she said, turning her back to her sister.

Caroline tried to do up the buttons with her eyes closed.

"Ouch!" said Martha. "You scratched me."

Caroline sighed and opened her eyes. Seven perfect blue buttons on a perfect blue dress stared at her. She concentrated on only one button at a time. Seven, six, five, four, three, two, one. She buttoned the last button and went downstairs without saying a word. She would have Mother button up her own dress.

"Why are you such a grouch, Caroline?" Martha called after her.

Caroline ignored her. There was something

in her that was making her be rude, and she could not stop it even if she wanted to. And she did not want to.

As Mother was buttoning up Caroline, Martha came downstairs. Caroline saw her feet first. And there, sticking out of a hole in her worn shoe, was Martha's stockinged toe. Caroline could see it poking out, like a squirrel sticking out of its hole in a tree. She felt a mean smile come onto her face, and said, "I do hope no one notices that big hole in your shoe, Martha."

Martha looked down at her shoe. She had not even noticed. Then she shrugged. "It's just a hole. No one notices shoes anyway."

Caroline had noticed. She said, "Well, it's too bad that you don't have nice shoes to match your dress." She looked at her own shoes, which had no holes in them.

"Don't be spiteful, Caroline," Mother said. Caroline bit her lip.

"Both of you go outside. The Carpenters are taking us to church in their wagon. I will be out with Eliza and Thomas in a minute."

Caroline saw Martha flush. She knew why. Charlie would be in the wagon. He would see Martha in her beautiful dress. But he also might see the hole in her shoe. That's why Martha flushed. It didn't matter if Martha's dress was new when her shoe had a hole in it. She followed Martha out to the wagon. She *hoped* Charlie would see Martha's toe.

Joseph and Henry were standing at the back of the wagon with Charlie. Charlie was older than Henry and younger than Joseph, but he was taller than both of them. He was talking loudly to Henry and Joseph, and his dark hair kept flopping over his forehead and into his eyes.

Caroline and Martha said good morning to Mr. and Mrs. Carpenter and joined the boys at the back of the wagon. Joseph jumped into the wagon and held out a hand for Caroline. She reached up and stepped onto the top of the wheel and over the side of the wagon back. She was careful at first not to get any splinters in her dress, but then she decided she didn't care. Maybe if her dress tore, Mother would make her a new one. But she landed safely in the back next to Joseph. Charlie helped Martha, who blushed as he took her hand, and Caroline noticed she tucked her feet under her as soon as she sat down. So Martha did care after all!

When Mother came out with Eliza and Thomas and everyone was settled, Mr. Carpenter made a loud clicking noise and rattled the reins. The horses snorted and jerked their heads. "Move along, boys," he said.

Caroline lifted her face to the clear sky and felt the sun warm her cheeks. Charlie was telling a story, but Caroline did not pay attention. She had to look around. The marsh marigolds brightened the fields along the sides of the road, and the cherry trees had burst into blossom. The sweet new smells of flowers and young grass blew through the air on the soft April wind. Spring was here to stay.

Soon the wagon stopped. The church was on top of a small hill. The summer before Father had died, he and Mr. Carpenter had worked with the townfolk to build this church. They cleared the land, cut the wood, hammered, and sawed from first light to last. The church grew and grew. They built the steeple tall and straight, and put in thick glass windows to catch and reflect the sun. They painted the walls and roof white, and made pews for everyone to sit on. Finally all that was left to do was put in the church bell, which had come all the way from Milwaukee. It was ringing now, saying, "Come to church. Come to church."

Everyone got out of the wagon. There were many people at the bottom of the hill, greeting one another for the first time since the winter. Under an oak tree halfway up the hill, were six girls Martha's age. They were town girls. They wore pretty pink and yellow dresses, white stockings, and shiny black shoes. Their hair ribbons matched their dresses, and they even had on white gloves. Caroline thought they looked beautiful.

"Let's go in now, children," Mother said.

Henry and Joseph went ahead with Mother, and Charlie joined his parents. Martha walked up the hill, with Caroline just behind her. As she neared the town girls, they giggled and pointed at her feet. Martha did not seem to notice, but Caroline had.

As Martha passed the town girls, one of them said to another in a loud whisper, "Poor country girl. Too bad she doesn't have new shoes to go with her new dress. I bet that dress came from a poor box sent by folks back East anyway. It looks too nice to be something that is really hers."

Martha stood stock-still. All the color drained from her face. When Caroline saw her sister silent, all of the hot, angry feelings evaporated. This was her sister, and no one could make fun of her.

Caroline marched right up to the girl who had spoken. The girl was so startled that she stepped backward and tripped, falling back on the dewy grass.

Caroline said, standing over her, "That *is* her dress, and we don't have any money for new shoes, but that doesn't make you any better than her."

The other girls clucked and squawked like chickens and huddled together clutching one another.

“Come on, Martha, let’s go to church,” said Caroline, grabbing her big sister’s hand. They walked away from the other girls.

“My dress is wet!” wailed the girl on the ground. “I can’t go to church like this!”

Caroline looked at Martha, and they laughed. Then they went into church, and held hands through the whole service.

When they returned home, Caroline told Mother every naughty thing that she had done. She had envied Martha for her new dress, she had not talked to Martha for almost a whole day, she had been glad that Martha had a hole in her shoe, and she had spoken back to a town girl. Mother was disappointed in Caroline, and Caroline was very ashamed of how she had treated Martha, and of caring so much about a silly dress. She did not mind Mother’s punishment of copying out five times the Bible verse *Do not rejoice when your enemies fall, and do not let your heart be glad when they stumble*. But she knew in her heart she still rejoiced over that town girl falling.

School

It was now time for Martha and Caroline to go to school. They took baths even though it wasn't Saturday. They scrubbed their skin until it glowed. They washed their hair and let it dry in the sun. Caroline had been looking forward to going to school all spring. But as each day brought them closer to the start of school for the summer, she started worrying. What if the other girls her age knew more than she did? She knew that there would be no big boys at school because they would be working in the fields, so she did not have to worry about someone like Danny McCarthy making trouble. But what if those town girls were there and made fun of her and Martha? What if the teacher was mean? What if she made no friends? When Mother woke up Caroline for the first day of school, Caroline's stomach was full of flutters.

"You've been waiting and waiting for your first day of school, Caroline," Mother said, "and you don't appear to be ill. Whatever is wrong?"

"I'm fine." Caroline looked away from Mother's eyes. "I feel tired, is all."

"A warm breakfast will surely cure that." Mother stood up. "Now hurry and dress, girls. There is still plenty to do before you get on your way to school."

"Yes ma'am," Caroline and Martha answered, jumping out of bed.

As Caroline got dressed, she wished that she and Martha were already walking home. Pulling her light blue dress over her petticoats, Caroline remembered that Mother had told them not to wear their aprons to school. She looked down at her blue dress and longed to wear her apron, if only to hide the faded fabric and the tiny stains that never went away, no matter how hard Mother scrubbed them on wash day.

"Mother says you're not yourself today," Grandma whispered in her ear as she pulled and twisted the three thick sections of Caroline's brown hair into a braid. "Can Grandma help?"

Looking up into Grandma's kind eyes, Caroline decided that it would be safe to tell Grandma about her worries. "I'm afraid to go to school, Grandma. I'm afraid of the schoolmaster."

"Why, that's just plain silliness, Caroline," Grandma said. Looking down at Caroline, her eyes were full of understanding. "If you are a good girl in school, as I am certain you will be, the schoolmaster will not find any need to discipline you. The schoolmaster will teach you to read and to spell. Anything you imagine beyond that is utter nonsense."

But Caroline still felt unsure. As she walked

with Martha down the road to school, her feet got slower and slower.

"Why are you walking so slowly?" said Martha. "We're going to be late for school!"

Caroline tried to make her feet go faster, but her legs felt heavy. At the far end of town, Caroline and Martha came to a large meadow that was edged with forest. The early summer breeze stirred the tall grass and wildflowers, rippling them in great waves. In the middle of the meadow was the schoolhouse. It looked like any other frame house, but here was the place that children went to learn as much as they could. Mother had gone to school, and her mother before her, and they had liked it. Martha had gone last year, and she had liked it, too. Caroline tried to concentrate on that as she and Martha got closer and closer. But she still had those worrying thoughts.

Boys who were too little to help in the fields were running around the front yard. There were girls of all ages, too. Caroline immediately saw the town girls standing together under a maple tree. They saw her and pointedly ignored her. Caroline felt relieved. That was the first worry gone.

A lady wearing a light gray dress with a full skirt walked out of the schoolhouse door. Her light straw-colored hair was wound in a bun. She rang the school bell.

"School is beginning, children," she called. "Everyone come inside." Her voice sounded kind, and she smiled as the children filed into the school. Caroline walked past her, knowing that this teacher would not be mean. That was a second worry gone.

Four rows of benches lined three sides of the room. The teacher's desk was up front, facing the benches. A black iron woodstove stood in the corner. It was used when the weather was cold. Now that the weather was warm, there was no fire in the woodstove.

"Let's sit next to a window, Caroline," said Martha.

Caroline and Martha slid into a bench, all the way over so other children could sit next to them. In a minute, a girl with curls all over her head sat with them. She seemed to be Caroline's age, and she looked very friendly. She smiled at Caroline, who smiled back. That was a third worry gone!

"Good morning, class." The teacher was in front of her desk. "My name is Miss Morgan, and I am your teacher. I am looking forward to teaching all of you. Education is a wonderful opportunity, and our country gives each of you an education to improve yourself. You must take every chance you can to come to school."

Caroline had no idea what Miss Morgan was saying. She had to go to school. Mother would not let her stay home.

Miss Morgan asked for each child's name and if that child knew how to read and write. She recorded the answers in a little black book. There were children who knew a lot more than Caroline. But there were also children like her who were still learning how to read and write. So that was the fourth and last worry gone!

Caroline was not nervous anymore. She would learn to read and write as well as Mother in this place. The mean town girls were there, but she did not have to talk to them. And there were plenty of girls who looked nice whom she could talk to. How could she have been scared? Caroline laughed at herself for all the worrying she had done. What a waste of good time. She realized that she was a very lucky girl to be at school, and began to understand a little bit of what Miss Morgan had said. Well, she would take every opportunity to improve herself. She bent her head over her primer and began to read.

HISTORY: IN CAROLINE'S TIME

SONG: "GREEN GROWS THE LAUREL"

GAME: POISON TAG

RECIPE: HOTCAKES WITH SUGAR SYRUP

PREVIEW OF *LITTLE TOWN AT THE CROSSROADS*

History

In Caroline's Time

Caroline was born in 1839 in Brookfield, Wisconsin. What else was happening in America around that time?

1839 • Abner Doubleday lays out the first baseball diamond in Cooperstown, New York, and then conducts the first game ever played

1840 • US Population: 17 million

1841 • William Henry Harrison, ninth US President, dies one month after inauguration; John Tyler becomes tenth President

1845 • James K. Polk inaugurated as 11th US President

1846 • Sewing machine patented by Elias Howe

1848 • Gold discovered in California

1849 • Zachary Taylor inaugurated as 12th US President
Walter Hunt invents the safety pin

1850 • President Zachary Taylor dies; Millard Fillmore becomes 13th US President
US Population: 21 million

Song

"Green Grows the Laurel"

Traditional Irish Folk Song

When Henry and Joseph had finished their game, Mother began to sing.

"Green grows the laurel, and so does the rue;
So woeful my love, at the parting with you.
But by the next morning our love we'll renew;
We'll change the green laurel to the orange and blue."

"Green Grows the Laurel" is an Irish folk song. The lyrics that Mother sings are slightly different from the traditional lyrics. This might be because the song was passed down to her through the generations.

Here are the traditional lyrics:

Green grows the laurel and soft falls the dew
Sad was my heart when I parted from you
And in our next meeting I hope you'll prove true
Never change the green laurel for the red, white,
and blue

I once had a sweetheart but now he is gone
He's gone and he's left me I'm here all alone
And since he has left me content I must be
I know he loves someone far better than me

I wrote him a letter so loving and kind
He wrote me another with sharp bitter lines
Saying, Keep your love letters and I will keep mine
And you write to your love and I'll write to mine

He passed by my window both early and late
And the looks that he gave me would make your
heart ache
The looks that he gave me ten thousand would kill
Wherever he wanders he'll be my love still

I once was as happy as the red blushing rose
But now I'm as pale as the lily that grows
Like the tree in the garden with its beauty all gone
Can't you see what I have come to from the loving
of one?

Game

Poison Tag

This is an outdoor game that was popular when Caroline was growing up. Now you can play it, too!

You'll need at least 3 players to play Poison Tag.

1. Designate a specific area where the game is to be played. Make sure there are clear boundaries. The smaller the area, the easier the game will be.
2. Decide who will be "it."
3. Have players stand in a circle a short distance away from the person who is "it."
4. Yell "Go!" to begin the game.
5. The person who is "it" will run after the other players and attempt to "tag" (touch) one of them. Yell, "Tag, you're it!" when you tag someone. That person immediately becomes it.
6. When a player is tagged, that player must hold on to the spot where they were tagged with one hand while running after the other players. For example, if you tag someone on their wrist, they must hold on to their wrist while they are "it," and can only let go after they have successfully tagged another player.

Recipe

Hotcakes with Sugar Syrup

Caroline waited impatiently, trying hard not to look at the tall, steaming stack of hotcakes. The very last thing Mother put on the table was the sugar syrup. Now they all sat down.

Now you can make Hotcakes with Sugar Syrup, just like Caroline.

To make Hotcakes you'll need:

4 cups All-Purpose Flour	*Extra Butter to Grease Griddle*
¾ Cup Sugar	*1 Large Egg*
2 Tablespoons Baking Powder	*2 Teaspoons Vanilla Extract*
2 Cups Milk	*2 Large Bowls*
8 Tablespoons Melted Unsalted Butter	*Griddle/Large Heavy Pan*

To make Sugar Syrup, you'll need:

2 Cups Water *2 Cups Sugar*
Saucepan

First make the Sugar Syrup:

1. Heat sugar and water together in a saucepan until the sugar dissolves.
2. Bring mixture to a boil and let boil for 4 minutes.
3. Remove from heat and let cool.

Then make the Hotcakes:

1. Stir the flour, sugar, and baking powder in a large bowl until mixed.
2. In another bowl, beat the milk, melted butter, egg, and vanilla until blended.
3. Pour wet ingredients into dry ingredients and beat until just blended (a few lumps are okay).
4. Heat griddle or large heavy pan over medium heat. Brush heated griddle/pan with a little butter.
5. Pour about ⅓ cup of batter for each hotcake, leaving a little space in between. Cook until golden brown underneath (you can lift up a corner to peek). Flip the hotcakes carefully and cook until the undersides are golden brown as well.
6. Repeat with rest of batter.
7. Serve hot with sugar syrup.

LITTLE TOWN AT THE CROSSROADS

by **MARIA D. WILKES**

Flags and Fifes

"If we don't hurry, Eliza, we're going to miss everything!" Caroline said, pulling her little sister's hand.

"The Glorious Fourth has barely begun!" Mother said. "Don't worry. We'll not miss the parade."

Brookfield was perfectly suited to greet the Glorious Fourth. Every road bustled with townsfolk dressed in their Sunday best heading to the crossroads of town to celebrate Independence Day. All five Quiner children's eyes grew wide as they took in the festivities, but Caroline thought she was the most excited.

This was her favorite holiday.

"Caroline and Martha, I need you to keep hold of Eliza and Thomas," Mother said, handing the babies to Caroline and her older sister. "As for you boys, Joseph and Henry-O, let's find a place for you to set down those picnic baskets. Mother Quiner, where would you like to sit?"

As Grandma scanned the crowded square, a loud noise right behind them made the whole family jump. *Zzzsss, pop! Zzzsss, bang!*

Grabbing Eliza, Caroline dashed to the side of the road as three sizzling firecrackers wriggled past and popped with a quick flip and tumble on the bumpy road ahead.

"No need to practice your jig 'fore tonight, little Brownbraid." Henry laughed out loud. "Those firecrackers won't hurt anybody."

From behind them, a friendly voice boomed almost as loud as the firecrackers. "Good morning, neighbors!"

Mr. Benjamin Carpenter was dressed in his finest Sunday suit. A brown beard covered his chin, and his long, thick brown hair was neatly combed and smoothed behind his ears.

"Can't recollect a prettier day for the Glorious Fourth. How 'bout you, little Brownbraid?" Mr. Carpenter asked Caroline.

"No, sir." Caroline was only six years old, and she couldn't remember many Fourth of Julys. All she recalled was the wonderful cheering and music.

Benjamin's wife, Sarah, beamed at Caroline, Eliza, and Martha. "You all look very pretty today."

"Thank you, ma'am," Caroline replied bashfully. Standing so close to Mrs. Carpenter, she couldn't help thinking that her own yellow church dress looked anything but pretty. Mrs. Carpenter's long-sleeved dress hugged her waist and ballooned into a wide, round skirt that swayed from side to side as she walked. Caroline looked up at Mother's simple black dress and silently wished that Mother could sometimes wear the beautiful dresses she worked so hard to make for other ladies in Brookfield.

Boom! Boom!

The maple leaves shook as a series of ear-splitting blasts pierced the air. Eliza clutched Caroline's hand. "What was that?" she cried.

"It's just a blast of gunpowder, little one," Mr. Carpenter explained.

"It means we're missing everything!" Caroline cried. "Let's go!"

The road grew even more crowded and noisy as they neared the crossroads of town. Up ahead, a fiddler fiddled and two lanky boys hopped and twirled and kicked their heels together in the air.

A stocky man with twirly whiskers had climbed onto a wide tree stump on the side of the road. "I stand here today, friends," he said, "to remind you it's been seventy years since we freed ourselves from the British! America is the greatest country on earth and we'll fight to keep it free till it's seven *hundred* and seventy years old!"

Caroline felt like shouting, too, but young ladies never shouted if they could help it. She remained quiet, but there was so much to feel proud of today.

When they had set down their picnic next to the Carpenters', Mother told Caroline and Martha they could find their friend Anna before dinner. "I bet she's still at the shop with her father," Caroline said, grabbing her sister's hand.

Caroline and Martha wove their way in and out among the townsfolk as they passed the tavern and the blacksmith's shop. All around, people chattered and laughed and greeted their neighbors with warm handshakes and hugs. Young children clung to their mothers' skirts while their older brothers tossed firecrackers and gobbled up handfuls of popcorn and their older sisters swung on tree swings and danced about the square. In front of every building, a cheery flag waved its stars and stripes in celebration.

Finally they arrived in front of the wheelwright's workshop.

"Hello, Anna!" Caroline called out to her friend as she peered inside the small building that Anna's father shared with the wagon maker. During the day, Joseph Short built cabinets and furniture in the shop. At night, he and Anna lived in the two rooms upstairs.

Anna's brown curls bounced about as she waved to Caroline and Martha. "Come! You must see what Papa is making!"

Stepping out of the bright sunlight into the dim shop, Caroline and Martha walked carefully around piles of wood, cabinets, tables, and chairs toward the back of the shop. Anna was leaning over her father's workbench as he whittled away at a small piece of wood.

"Look! Papa's making me a fife!" Anna said exuberantly.

"Mornin', Miss Caroline, Miss Martha," Anna's father greeted them in his heavy Scottish burr.

"Good morning, sir," Caroline and Martha answered politely.

Mr. Short pushed a handful of dark curls out of his eyes and glanced over at his daughter. "Be kind and share with your friends, eh, darlin' Anna?"

"Of course, Papa," Anna replied. "Is it finished yet?"

"Try." Mr. Short handed Anna the instrument and watched as she lifted it to her lips.

Anna's cheeks grew even more round and pink as she blew over the tiny holes as hard as she could. High-pitched squeaks and squeals skirted from one side of the shop to the other.

"It's perfect!" Caroline clapped.

"Blow softer, Anna," Mr. Short suggested. "The sound will be much prettier."

"Yes, Papa," Anna replied happily.

"Come, girls. I hear the parade." Mr. Short smiled.

Leading the girls back through the front room, he stood beside the door as they stepped into the brilliant sunshine. Caroline caught her breath as a giant flag marched toward them, a swaying wave of red, white, and blue pointing toward the heavens. A long line of men marched close behind, their trumpets and bugles blasting merrily. Still others followed, tapping, snapping, and booming their drums in response to the bugles' triumphant song.

"There are Henry and Joseph and Charlie!" Martha cried. "There, with the drummers!"

"The fifes and flutes are coming next, Anna." Mr. Short pointed toward the end of the parade, where another group of men, blowing a lilting, joyous melody, was surrounded by children of all sizes, who marched and skipped along. "Go now! You girls should march, too."

So they marched through town, music blaring and flags waving all around them.

"Hail! Columbia, happy land!
Hail! Ye heroes, heav'n-born band!
Who fought and bled in Freedom's cause,
Let independence be our boast
Ever mindful what it cost
Ever grateful for the prize
Let its altar reach the skies."

Caroline didn't know every word, but she hummed along as best she could. The parade finally passed the crossroads of town, and Caroline saw Mother, Grandma, and the Carpenters on the side of the road, waving as they sang the final refrain:

"Firm, united, let us be,
Rallying round our liberty;

As a band of brothers join'd,
Peace and safety we shall find."

As the parade ended, Caroline decided she was very, very glad to be independent and free. If only they could celebrate their freedom more than one day a year!

Spelling Bee

For days following the Glorious Fourth, Caroline felt the rush of having marched in her first parade. She hadn't wanted it to be over, so she kept marching all around the frame house, holding an imaginary fife to her lips and humming "Yankee Doodle." She marched while she pushed chairs to the table before every meal, she marched as she carried clean, dry dishes back to the dish dresser, she marched while she swept up the bedroom. She marched swiftly past Joseph and Henry splitting logs by the woodpile, dodging the stray chunks of wood spinning through the air. She marched as she tossed handfuls of oats and corn to the hens scratching and pecking at the dirt around her feet. She marched to school, which got on Martha's nerves, but Charlotte didn't care.

"Will you stop!" her sister said. "You can march again next year in the parade."

But Caroline wouldn't stop. She marched to her bench at school and saluted Anna, who was sitting next to her. She thought she'd march everywhere.

One morning in school, Caroline's teacher, Miss Morgan, called her to the front of the room. "Caroline Quiner, please come to the front of the room," she said. "I'd like you to represent the first primer students today in the spelling bee."

That was enough to stop Caroline in her tracks. Of course, she had studied her spelling words, but never before had she been called to the head of the class. She stood up and hastily smoothed her faded red dress over her petticoats. She smiled thinly at Anna and slowly walked—not marched—to the front of the room.

As she passed the eight rows of benches packed with girls of all ages and sizes and dotted with a handful of the youngest boys from town, Caroline wished that her stomach would stop flip-flopping. She had recited her spelling words to Mother and Grandma every day for a week. She knew each word by heart, but she was still afraid that she'd forget all her spellings the moment she opened her mouth to recite them in front of the whole class.

Nearing the front of the room, Caroline also began wishing that she had worn her other dress. It wasn't nearly so faded as the one she was wearing. The tiny white dots had practically disappeared into the fabric, and the once-cheerful red color had become a tired pink. Caroline took her place in line.

LITTLE HOUSE

LITTLE HOUSE. BIG ADVENTURE.

Little House [in the Highlands]

It's 1788, and Ma[rtha lives in a] house in Glencaraid, Scotland. Martha's father is Laird Glencaraid, and the life of a laird's daughter is not always easy for a lively girl like Martha. She would rather be running barefoot through the fields of heather than acting like a proper lady! But between lessons, Martha always finds time to play on the rolling Scottish hills.

[Little House i]n Brookfield

[...]e Quiner lives in the bustling frontier town of Brookfield, Wisconsin. It's been one whole year since Caroline's father was lost at sea, and every member of her family must pitch in to help with the farm chores. With trips to town, getting through the first frost, and starting school, Caroline is busy discovering new things every day!

Little House by Boston Bay

It's 1814, and Charlotte lives with her family near the city of Boston. What an exciting time she has! There's Mama's garden to tend to, Papa's blacksmith shop to visit, and lots of brothers and sisters to play with. Best of all, Charlotte is a brand-new American girl, born just one generation after the United States of America was formed.

Little House on Rocky Ridge

It's 1893, and Rose and her parents, Laura and Almanzo, are moving to Missouri, the land of the Big Red Apple. They say good-bye to Ma and Pa Ingalls and Laura's sisters, and set off for the lush green valleys of the Ozarks. The journey is long and holds many adventures along the way which they hope will lead them to a new home and a new life.

HarperCollins*Children'sBooks*

www.littlehousebooks.com